# Rolf Heimann's

# UltiMaze
## BOOK

Troll

**Thirteen Amazing Mazes** for the Novice,
Seasoned or Master Maze-Solver

For my little helpers, Elisa and Vinny

First published in USA by Troll Communications L.L.C.

Copyright © 1992 Rolf Heimann

Design by Debra Billson

Printed in USA.

ISBN 0-8167-3699-5
10 9 8 7 6 5 4 3 2 1

# Introduction

In the pages that follow, you will find 13 of the most challenging mazes ever collected between the covers of one book. You will notice that they become more difficult as you advance through the book (even a knowledge of Latin might help you out sometimes!), but once you find the hidden key, you should be able to unlock the secret of every maze.

Each maze is totally different from the next, and each has its own set of rules. For instance:

Stay on the yellow path, but don't cross any lines!

Find the correct ladder, grab the snake's tail and follow it to the head. Then find the ladder to the next snake's tail ... and on you go.

Stick to the water and you won't run aground.

······ Can you figure out how the two tugboats are connected? ····

Even though the mazes all look different, they do have something in common. All start on the middle left and finish on the middle right, and, if you look carefully, all the objects pictured below are hidden in each maze. And if you get lost, you can always cheat and look at the solutions at the back of the book.

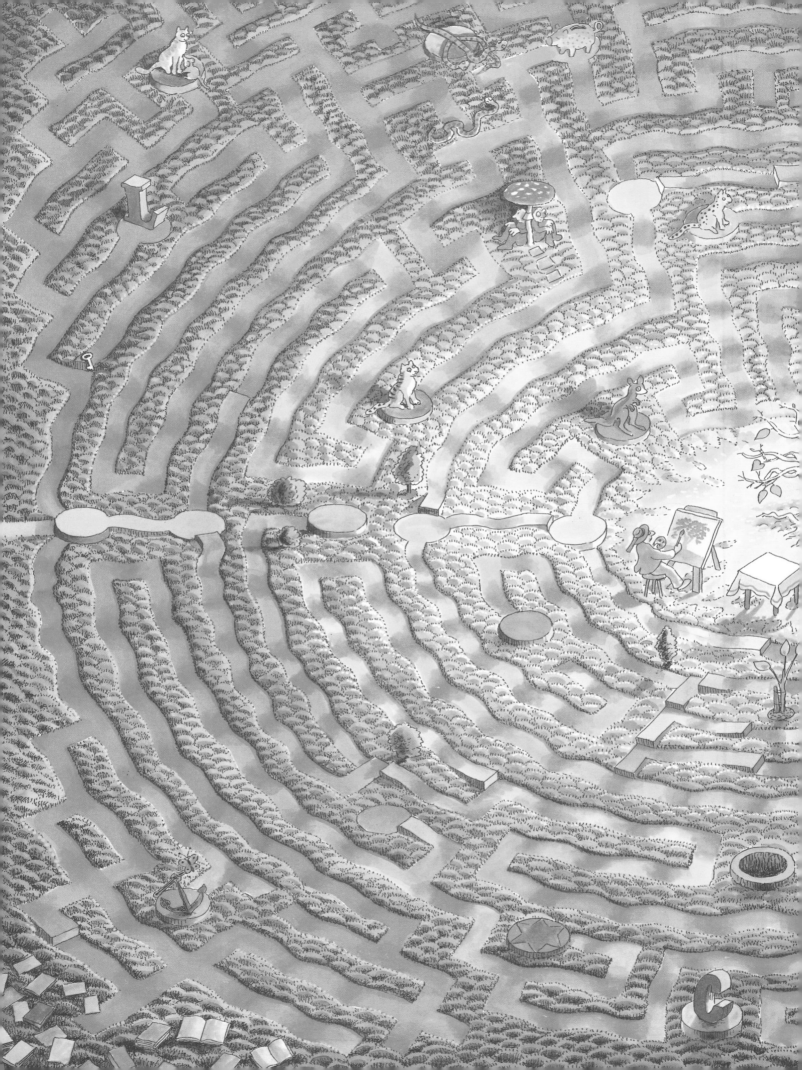

PELEGANUS

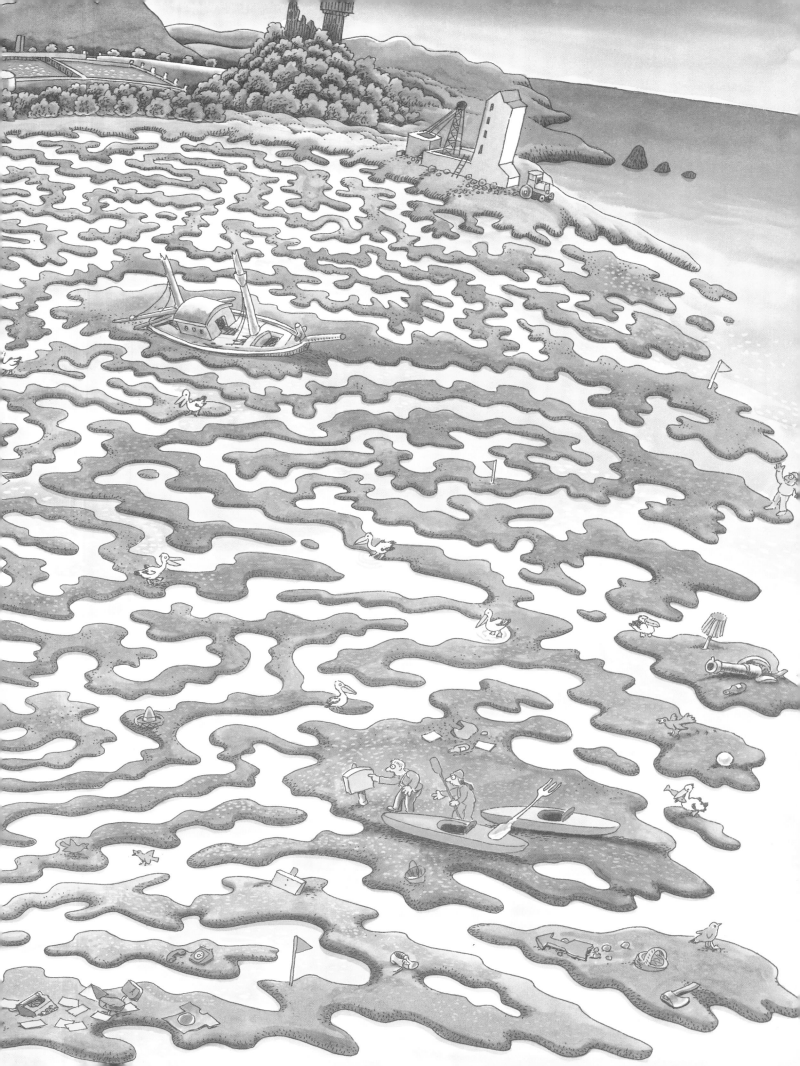

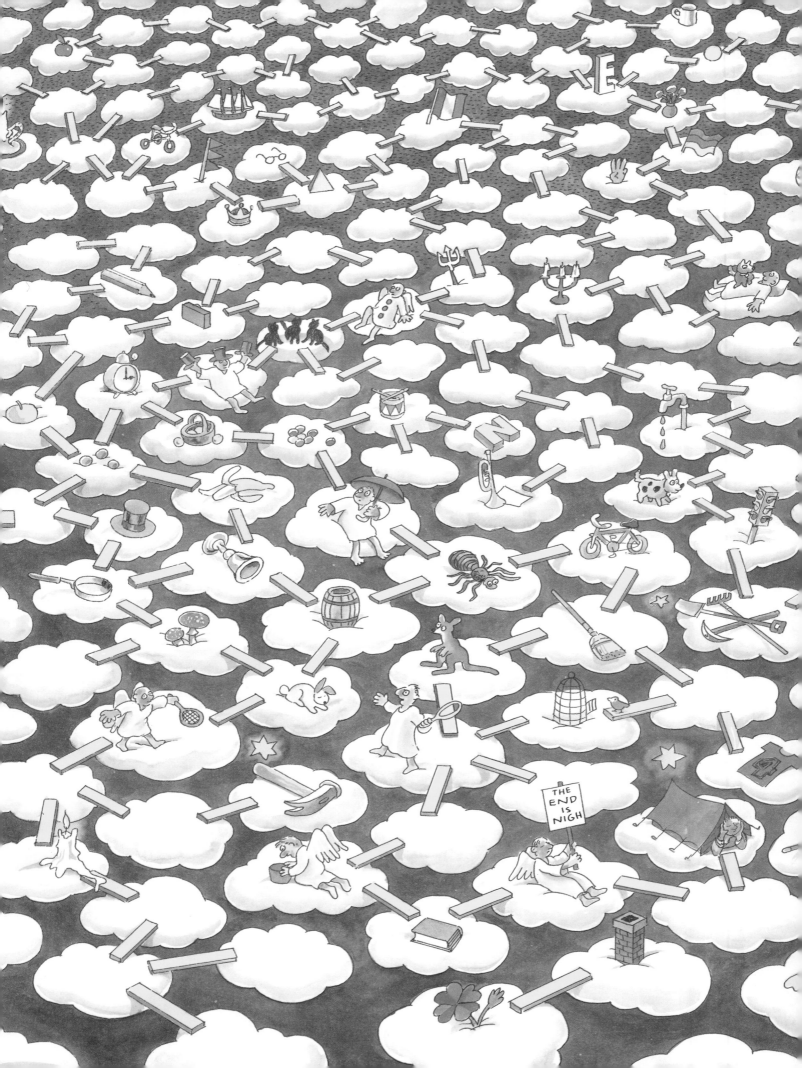

# The solutions

The key is lying on a step. Whenever you come to a step, go up!

*Pelecanus* is the key word – Latin for pelican, of course! These friendly birds will guide you through.

Number 3 is the key to this maze. Follow a path over the clouds that relate to the number 3: 3 balls, 3 o'clock, 3 hats . . .

This one was a little difficult, wasn't it? *Omnibus Idem* is the key, and these letters in sequence spell out the correct path. *Omnibus Idem* is Latin for "To all the same." Didn't you know that?

The key to this one is as simple as ABC. The maze isn't hard to follow, but could you find all the objects that mark the alphabet along the way? Some of them are: Abraham, balloon, the musical note 'C', diesel or Danish flag, Escher or energy (E=mc2), French or fork, Greenpeace, hexagon (on front of car), Inquisition or insect, Joseph (and the coat of many colors), koala, lighthouse, Mercedes star, Nixon or Napoleon, Om, Picasso or paddle boat, Qantas, robot, Stalin or sphinx, Tower Bridge or Tyrannosaurus Rex, UFOs, volcano, windmill, xenophobe, yacht or yucca trees and zebras or Zen and the art of motorcycle maintenance.

Blue, white and red are the colors of the French flag. Go from the blue ladder to the white snake to the red ladder to the blue snake, and so on.

In this one, the key in the right margin is half blue and half pink. These colors will guide you through, so try to keep between them.

The clue is the caterpillar on the key. Follow the nibbled leaves!

The eyes have it! The key is carried by the fish with the colorful scales. All you have to do is match the colored scales with the same colored eyes and you will be on the right track.

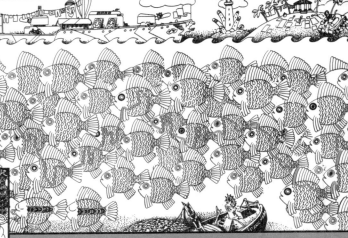

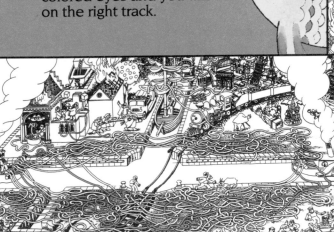

Two men pulling at a green loop have the key. The tugboats are joined because the green rope connects the two red ropes.

Karl Marx has the key around his neck, so it must be obvious that whenever you come to a corner you must turn left, not right!

If you can use a map, you should be able to solve this maze. The key directs you to a small map of the way through the maze.

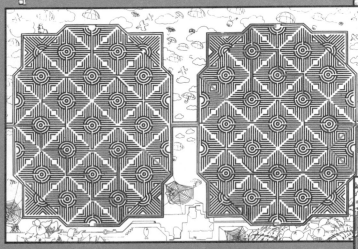

The year 1945 is the key here. At the end of World War 2, in 1945, Dresden was destroyed by bombs. The numbers on the left-hand side of the maze, when followed through the 1-9-4-5 sequence, should help you on the way.

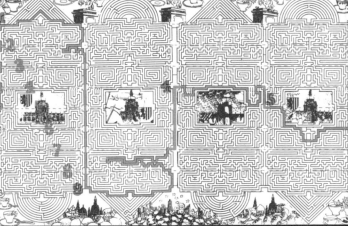